**12** huia birds greet a new day,
in songs that sweetly share the word.
With orange cheeks and funny-shaped beaks,
they are a beautiful sight to be heard.

**12** huia birds, midnight black
from head to tails tipped white.
Bright flashes streak to the forest floor,
down from the treetops' height.

He chisels old logs, as she probes the ground.
Their favourite food is the huhu grub,
and there is plenty to go around.

This is life in the forest,
as ancient as night and day.
Time just flows on forever —
it has always been this way.

Until one day, out of the blue,
on the horizon, a single canoe.
People arrive to stake their claim,
life in the forest will never be the same.

**11** huia birds,
gathering stuff for their nests.
Down on the forest floor,
not used to unwelcome guests.

Along slinks a dog,
invading their space,
'I smell something
to hunt down and chase.'

**10** huia birds,
excited before the rain.
All kinds of food appear
in their drenched domain.

A rat scuttles into view,
he sniffs the air and squeaks,
'So many tasty huia!
I'll be feasting for weeks.'

**9** huia birds,
snuggling in branches above.
Giving their sweet calls
and singing songs of love.

Along he comes, the supreme chief;
only he can wear prized huia feathers.
'This wooden case has been specially carved
to carry such valued treasures.'

As ship after ship sets anchor in the bay,
people spill over this land of forest green.
They are the strangest creatures
that these birds have ever seen.

**8** huia birds
nesting in the night,
content beneath the moon
with its pale blue light.

One hungry possum
drops by without a sound.
'Huia chicks are delicious
and there are lots to go around.'

**7** huia birds,
their chorus fading as they sing.
They make up in spirit
what they have lost in numbering.

Along prowls a cat
to poke at the nest.
'In the forest you may be king,
but I'll show you who's really best.'

**6** huia birds,
always in pairs and forever loyal.
The locals crown them king of the forest birds,
revering them as royal.

A weasel clambers into view,
with his good friends stoat and ferret,
'These birds have had their day by now,
their kingdom is ours to inherit.'

**5** huia birds,
squeezed into their lonely lowland home.
Their neighbourhood is shrinking fast,
with nowhere else to roam.

Settlers come with fire,
to burn the forest down,
'Nothing must get in the way
of building our new town.'

**4** huia birds
flee to the misty hills.
Soft flute songs of loss and sadness
warble from their bills.

From the mist appears
a man of science
who studies birds by trade.
'Rare creatures like these
don't belong in the wild,
but in museums, displayed.'

**3** huia birds
hanging on at the brink.
They've been here as long as life itself,
will they disappear in just a blink?

Along comes a chief,
to save the huia before they've vanished.
Finally, a law is passed
so that hunting them is banished.

**2** huia birds
perch up in a tree.
Warbling a chirpy song,
happy as can be.

For two huia birds,
life can start anew …

Until one day, a ship arrives out of the blue.

A duke comes ashore and is presented with a gift. When a huia feather is placed in his hat — hunting resumes forthwith.

**2** huia birds
cling together as night falls.
Ivory bills groom each other
with low, loving calls.

Along stalk hunters,
full of passion,
'White-tipped tail feathers,
are the latest fashion.'

1 huia bird in a cage,
calling out for her mate.
It's nesting season,
she hopes he won't be late.

Along trot lords and ladies
in their boots and spats,
'We must have those feathers
in the headbands of our hats.'

As they open the cage and reach for her tail,
the huia doesn't squeak, squawk or cry.
Instead she hops through a gap,
flies up and around ...

Then she vanishes from sight, off into the sky.

Now they're nothing but a memory.
But look around and you might see …

**12** huia birds, alive and well,
in paintings, songs
and stories we tell.

Stories such as this give voice
to the song of the huia bird.
With orange cheeks and funny-shaped beaks,
they were a beautiful sight to be heard.